NODDY

Book 3

Once Noddy was asked to a party. Sally Skittle asked him, and Noddy was very pleased.

"I'm going to Sam Skittle's party," he told Big-Ears. "His mother asked me if I would. It's his birthday."

"Then you must take him a present," said Big-Ears. "Have you any money in your money-box, Noddy?"

"Oh yes, lots!" said Noddy. "I was saving up to buy myself a nice pair of warm gloves, Big-Ears. My hands do get so cold on these winter days, when I'm driving the car."

Big-Ears tipped out the money from the money-box. "Yes," he said, "you've quite a lot. You can buy the gloves and a present for Sam Skittle, too."

So Noddy bought Sam Skittle a little trumpet, and he bought himself a pair of fine red gloves, very warm indeed.

He felt very proud when he put them on. They were the first pair he had had. He thought he would wear them to the party and drive himself there in his little car.

"Now—am I all clean and tidy?" he said to himself when the party afternoon came. "Have I washed my hands and face? Yes, I have. Have I brushed my hair? Yes—oh no, I haven't. Dear me, what a good thing that I ask myself questions like these!"

He brushed his hair. He put on his hat, and the little bell jingled merrily. He tied up his shoe-laces well and brushed some dust off his shorts. He put on his nice new gloves and went out to his car.

"I've got new gloves that fit my wooden hands nicely,"
said Noddy to his car.

"Parp-parp!" said the car, and off they went. They came
to Sally Skittle's house and Noddy got out and went in at
the gate—and, dear me, on the path was an ENORMOUS
puddle left by the rain! Noddy stepped right into it. Splash!

"Oh—how wet my shoes are!" he said. "What will Sally
Skittle say!"

Sally Skittle scolded him. "Dear dear! To think you didn't see a puddle as big as that!" she said. "And will you believe it, Gilbert Golly has done just the same, and so has Billy Bear! Take off your shoes, and I will dry them. Give me your gloves, too, and I will put them with your shoes."

So Noddy, Gilbert Golly and Billy Bear didn't wear any shoes at the party, but they enjoyed it all the same. The floor was nice and slippery and the three of them slid up and down.

The tea was lovely, and the cake was lovely too—the candles were made in the shape of skittles, and that made everyone laugh.

Sam Skittle liked the trumpet that Noddy brought him. Sally Skittle, his Mother, said that he liked it too much, because he wouldn't stop blowing it!

Noddy was sorry when it was time to go home. "I like the beginning of a party, and I like the middle, but I don't like the end," he said. "Why don't we have parties with only beginnings and middles, Sally Skittle?"

"Now, don't you begin asking me silly questions like Sam," said Sally. "Look, go and find your shoes, Noddy. There they are, over there, with your red gloves."

Gilbert Golly had put his on already. Billy Bear said he couldn't be bothered.

Noddy put on the red shoes with blue laces. He didn't put on his gloves till he had shaken hands with Sally Skittle.

"Thank you very much for having me," he said. "I have had a lovely time."

Then out he went to his little car. He put on his gloves, and off he went.

But after a little while Noddy thought there was something wrong with his gloves. They kept slipping off his hands! And then, dear me, one of his feet slid out of a shoe. What was the matter?

Noddy stopped the car and got out. He put on the shoe again—but his foot seemed much too small for it! No wonder it slipped off—and, goodness, his hands were much too small for his gloves, too!

"I'm going small!" suddenly wailed Noddy. "Somebody's put a spell on me! I'm going smaller and smaller, I know I am! Soon I'll be so small that I won't be seen—and then what shall I do! I'll go and tell Big-Ears!"

So he got into his car again and drove at top speed to Big-Ears' little toadstool house. He jumped out of his car and ran to Big-Ears' door, one of his shoes falling off as he ran.

"Big-Ears! Big-Ears! Something dreadful is happening!" wailed Noddy, knocking at the door. "I'm going small. Ever

so small. Look at my new gloves—they just won't keep on
my hands—and look at my feet! My shoes won't stay on!"

"Good gracious! This is dreadful!" said Big-Ears in alarm.
"But wait—your hat still fits your head! You can't be going
small. Give me one of the shoes, Noddy."

Noddy gave him one, and after one look at it Big-Ears began to laugh and laugh. "Oh, Noddy! HOW silly you are! These are Billy Bear's shoes. Look, his name is inside—and his gloves, too! He has enormous feet and paws—so, of course, his gloves and shoes don't fit you!"

Dear me, Noddy was so very, very glad! And see, off he goes to Mrs. Tubby Bear's to get back his own shoes and gloves. He isn't going small after all!

TOM KITTEN'S TRICK

One day Noddy thought he would go fishing and catch a big fish for his dinner.

"Then I will ask Big-Ears and Tessie Bear to dinner with me, and I shall feel very proud!" said Noddy. "I will go and ask Big-Ears now."

So he went knocking at Big-Ears' toadstool house. "Big-Ears—please come to dinner with me today. I am going to catch a big fish."

He asked little Tessie Bear too, and she was very pleased. "I'll come," she said. "And I'll help cook the dinner."

Well, Noddy set off with his rod and line, and soon he came to a big round pond. "I shall catch my fish here," he said, and he sat down on the bank and began to fish.

Soon along came little Tom Kitten and he grinned at Noddy. "There's no fish in that pond!" he said.

"You don't know anything about it!" said Noddy. "Go away. You're always teasing people."

"Big-Ears is looking for you," said Tom Kitten. "He's over there."

Noddy put down his rod and ran to find Big-Ears at once. Naughty Tom grinned. He knew that Big-Ears wasn't anywhere near—he just wanted to play a little trick on Noddy!

Do you know what he did? He had seen an old boot in the pond, and he quickly waded in and what did he do but fix that boot to the end of Noddy's line! How he laughed!

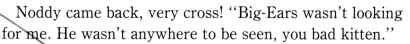

Noddy came back, very cross! "Big-Ears wasn't looking for me. He wasn't anywhere to be seen, you bad kitten."

He picked up his rod—and dear me, he felt something on the end of the line at once! "A fish! I've got a fish!" he cried. "My goodness me, it's a BIG one!"

Noddy pulled and pulled, trying to bring up the big fish—and at last up it came. There was the boot, dangling on the end of his line.

Tom Kitten rolled over and over on the grass and laughed till he cried. "Ho-ho-ho! *I* put it there! You thought it was a great big fish! Oh, what a tale. I'll tell everyone in the village!"

"You're very unkind," said Noddy. "I thought it was such a big fish—and I was going to cook it for dinner and I've asked Big-Ears and Tessie Bear . . ."

"Ho, ho, ho!" laughed Tom Kitten. "I'll go and tell them they'll have fried boot for dinner, with boot-lace sauce!"

"Hallo—what's all this noise about?" suddenly said a voice, and up came big Mr. Burly Bear. "Why, little Noddy—I *do* believe you've caught the boot I lost in the pond last winter when I skated on it and the ice broke! I fell in and lost one of my boots—and here it is back again! I shall dry it out and wear it again. Noddy, you really are very, very clever!"

"Am I?" said Noddy, and his head nodded up and down fast because he was very pleased.

"You are," said Mr. Burly Bear. "Look, here is ten pence for catching my boot. You go and buy a fish at the fishmonger's and give a little party."

"Oh, *thank you*!" cried Noddy. "I'll go this very minute. Ha, ha, Tom Kitten—you played a trick on me, but *you're* the one that looks silly now!"

And off he went to buy a nice big fish for dinner.

Look—he's in his little house cooking it now, with little Tessie Bear to help him, and Big-Ears is laying the table.

"We're going to have a very nice time," said Noddy. "And all because I caught a boot instead of a big fish!"

NODDY AND THE WOODEN HORSE

Now once when Noddy was driving along a country road his car suddenly made a peculiar noise, and then stopped.

"Good gracious! What's wrong with you?" said Noddy, in alarm, and he got out to see. "Your wheels haven't got a puncture, you've plenty of petrol. Then WHY don't you go?"

"Parp-parp," said the car, dolefully, and gave a little rattle.

"I'll have to take you to the garage and get you mended," said Noddy. "Something has gone wrong. But, dear me, I'll have to push you all the way because this is a very lonely place and there's nobody to help me."

So he began to push and push, and how he panted and puffed. "I sound like an engine going up a hill!" said Noddy. "Oh dear, I shall never get you to the garage!"

He pushed the car round a corner of the lane, and then he suddenly heard a noise. ''Hrrrrrumph! Help! Hrrrrumph!''

"Now what can *that* be?" said Noddy, and he stood and listened.

"Nay-hay-hay-hay-hay! Hrrrrrumph! Help!"

"Why—it's a horse in trouble!" said Noddy, and he squeezed through the hedge to find it. Sure enough, in the field beyond was a small horse, neighing and snorting loudly.

"What's the matter?" called Noddy.

"I walked into this muddy bit," said the horse, "and look—my front legs have sunk down into the mud and I can't get them out!"

Noddy ran to him. "I'll pull you out!" he said. "What part
of you shall I pull?"

"My tail," said the horse. "It's a very strong tail. Hold hard—pull. PULL! Pull HARDER. I'm coming. I'm coming!"

Noddy pulled hard at the wooden horse's tail, and, quite suddenly, the horse's front legs came out of the mud, and the horse sat down hard on Noddy.

"Oooh, don't!" said Noddy. "I'm squashed to nothing. Get up, wooden horse. Don't sit on me like this."

"Sorry," said the horse, and got up. "You are really very kind. It was lucky for me that you came by just then in your car."

"Yes, it was," said Noddy. "But I wasn't *in* my car. Something's gone wrong with it, and I've got to push it all the way into Toyland Village. Goodness, I shall be tired!"

"You needn't be," said the wooden horse. "I am quite used to pulling carts. I could pull your car for you, if you like, all the way to the garage! I'd be glad to do you a good turn, little Noddy."

"Oh *thank* you!" said Noddy. "How lucky I am! Come along—I'll get my ropes and tie you to the car. What fun!"

And now, there goes Noddy sitting in his car steering it carefully, and the little wooden horse is walking in front, pulling it well. How everyone stares!

"Aren't I lucky?" calls little Noddy. "My car broke
down—and I found a little wooden horse to pull it!"

"You *are* lucky, Noddy—but, you see, you're kind too,
and kind people are *always* lucky!"